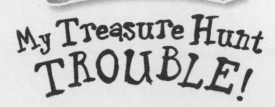

My Treasure Hunt TROUBLE!

Betty G. Birney worked at Disneyland
and the Disney Studios, has written many
children's television shows and is the author
of over forty books, including the bestselling
The World According to Humphrey, which won
the Richard and Judy Children's Book Club
Award, *Friendship According to Humphrey*, *Trouble
According to Humphrey*, *Surprises According to
Humphrey* and *More Adventures According to
Humphrey*. Her work has won many awards,
including an Emmy and three Humanitas
Prizes. She lives in America with her husband.

Have you read all of Humphrey's adventures?
The World According to Humphrey
Friendship According to Humphrey
Trouble According to Humphrey
Adventure According to Humphrey
(special publication for World Book Day 2008)
Surprises According to Humphrey
More Adventures According to Humphrey
Holidays According to Humphrey
School According to Humphrey
Mysteries According to Humphrey
Humphrey's Big-Big-Big Book of Stories (3 books in 1)
Humphrey's Great-Great-Great Book of Stories (3 books in 1)

Humphrey's Book of Fun-Fun-Fun
Humphrey's Ha-Ha-Ha Joke Book
Humphrey's World of Pets

Humphrey's Tiny Tales
My Pet Show Panic!
My Treasure Hunt Trouble!
My Summer Fair Surprise!
My Creepy-Crawly Camping Adventure!
My Great Big Birthday Bash!

By the same author
The Princess and the Peabodys

My Treasure Hunt TROUBLE!

BETTY G. BIRNEY

Illustrated by Penny Dann

faber and faber

First published in 2011
by Faber and Faber Limited
Bloomsbury House, 74–77
Great Russell Street, London WC1B 3DA
This edition first published in 2012

Printed in England by CPI Group (UK) Ltd, Croydon, CR0 4YY

A CIP record for this book
is available from the British Library

ISBN 978–0–571–28243–2

4 6 8 10 9 7 5 3

Welcome to
MY WORLD

Hi! I'm Humphrey. I'm lucky to be the classroom hamster in Room 26 of Longfellow School. It's a big job because I have to go home with a different student each weekend and try to help my friends. Luckily, my cage has a lock-that-doesn't-lock, so I can get out and have BIG-BIG-BIG adventures!

I'd like you to meet some of my friends

Og

a frog, is the other classroom pet in Room 26. He makes a funny sound: BOING!

Lower-Your-Voice-A.J.

has a loud voice and calls me Humphrey Dumpty.

Wait-For-The-Bell Garth

is A.J.'s best friend – and a great friend of mine, too!

Andy

Garth's little brother. He calls me 'ham'.

Golden-Miranda

has golden hair, like I do. She also has a dog named Clem. Eeck!

Speak-Up-Sayeh

is unsqueakably smart, but she's shy and doesn't like to speak in class.

Stop-Giggling-Gail

loves to giggle – and so do I!

Sit-Still-Seth

is always on the move.

I think you'll like my other friends, too, such as *Repeat-It-Please-Richie, Pay-Attention-Art, Raise-Your-Hand-Heidi* and *Don't-Complain-Mandy*.

CONTENTS

1 Secret Treasure   1

2 The Trouble Begins   18

3 The Hunt is On   43

4 Mystery Solved   58

Secret Treasure

'Can you keep a secret, Humphrey?' Garth whispered.

'Of course,' I whispered back.

But since I'm a hamster and Garth is a human, all he heard was 'Squeak!'

'How about you, Og?' Garth asked my friend.

Og answered 'BOING!' because he

is a frog who makes a VERY-VERY-VERY strange sound.

'There's going to be a treasure hunt in my garden tomorrow,' Garth said. 'But it's a secret. Don't tell anybody, okay?'

'Eeek!' I squeaked. I wasn't sure what a treasure hunt was, but it sounded exciting.

'BOING-BOING!' Og splashed around in his tank.

'I've worked out some of the clues already,' Garth said. 'And I haven't even told A.J.'

A.J. was Garth's best friend. They were both in my class at Longfellow School.

I'm the classroom hamster in Room 26. Og is the classroom frog.

It's part of my job to go home with a different student each weekend.

Frogs can go for several days without food, so Og usually stays back in Room 26. But this weekend Garth invited everyone in our class to a party, including Og and me. Our teacher, Mrs Brisbane, said we could both go, which made me unsqueakably happy.

My cage and Og's tank sat on the desk in Garth's room. We watched as he cut paper into squares.

'The clues should be hard,' he said. 'But not too hard. After all, somebody has to find the treasure.'

'What's the treasure?' I asked,
wishing Garth could understand me.

Garth stopped cutting paper and
looked at me.

'Thanks, Humphrey,' he said. 'You gave me an idea for a great place to hide it!'

'You're welcome,' I squeaked. 'But what *is* the treasure?'

'BOING!' Og said.

As Garth began writing on the squares of paper, I thought about TREASURE-TREASURE-TREASURE! I knew that treasure was something special, like gold and silver coins. Or sparkly jewels.

In the books Mrs Brisbane read to us in class, people were always looking for treasure. Sometimes treasure was buried in the ground. Sometimes it was at the bottom of the sea.

I scurried to the side of my cage
near Og's tank.

'What kind of treasure would you
like?' I asked him.

Og just stared at me with his goofy
eyes. I didn't think coins or jewels
would be of much use to a frog. He'd
probably rather have crickets or flies.
Ewww!

Coins or jewels wouldn't be of use to
a hamster, either, but I still wanted to
go on the treasure hunt.

Suddenly, a small voice called out, 'Ham!'

Garth's little brother, Andy, raced into the room and headed for my cage.

'He's a hamster, not a ham,' Garth said.

'Ham!' Andy shouted.

I don't like being called a 'ham', but, to be fair, Andy is quite small.

Andy pointed at the squares of paper. 'What's that?'

'That's where I'm writing down clues for the treasure hunt,' Garth explained.

'What's that?' Andy asked.

'It's a game where my friends have to follow clues and see who can find the treasure first,' Garth said.

'What's that?' Andy asked, pointing at Og.

'That's Og the frog,' Garth said.

'Now be quiet so I can write out the clues.'

'What's—' said Andy.

Garth put his finger to his lips and said, 'Sssh!'

Andy put his finger to his lips and said, 'Sssh!' too.

Garth wrote something on one of the squares.

'Frog,' Andy said.

He stared hard at Og. Og stared right back.

'BOING!' Og said in his funny voice.

'Sssh!' Andy said.

Og leaped into the water with a huge splash.

Garth sighed.

'Mum!' he called. 'Can you get Andy out of here? He's bothering me.'

Garth's mum appeared at the door. 'Let Andy help. He wants to be included in the party.'

'I can't write out the clues with him here,' Garth complained.

'You can only stay if you watch quietly,' Garth's mum told Andy.

She put her finger to her lips and said, 'Sssh!'

'Okay,' the little boy answered. 'Sssh!'

At first, Andy watched quietly as Garth began writing on the slips of paper.

'What rhymes with flower?' Garth asked.

'BOING!' Og said.

Poor Og. Doesn't he know that BOING doesn't rhyme with flower at all?

'Shower! That works,' Garth said.

I was trying to think of a flower that showered when Andy asked, 'What's that?'

'A clue,' Garth told him. 'Like a riddle.'

'Widdle,' Andy said.

Aha! A clue is like a riddle! I like riddles. I was unsqueakably curious about these clues.

Garth wrote some more and then asked me, 'What do you think of this clue?' and he read it out loud:

'Everyone knows you must water a flower. Tip me over, I'll give it a shower.'

'GREAT-GREAT-GREAT!' I squeaked. I had no idea what the answer to the riddle was.

As Garth wrote, he muttered other strange words, like 'frown' and 'goal' and 'basket'.

Then he opened a desk drawer and pulled out a treasure chest so small that he could hold it in the palm of his hand. Still, it looked like a real treasure chest and it even had a tiny lock on it.

'What's that?' Andy said.

'It's the treasure for the treasure hunt. It's something anyone in Room 26 would love to have,' Garth said.

Anyone? Even a hamster?

'Remember, this is a secret,' he

added. 'Do you promise not to tell anyone?'

'Promise,' Andy said.

'Promise,' I squeaked.

'BOING!' Og agreed.

To my surprise, Garth opened the door to my cage!

Then he carefully put the treasure chest inside, covering it over with my bedding.

'You leave it right there,
Humphrey,' he said. 'And don't peek.'

'Okay,' I promised.

But even as I said it, I knew it
would be a hard promise to keep.

The Trouble Begins

'A.J.'s here,' Garth's dad called from the hallway.

Garth quickly hid all of the pieces of paper in his desk drawer.

'He's spending the night,' he explained. 'But don't tell him about the treasure hunt.'

'Okay,' Andy said. 'Sssh!'

A.J. raced into the room. 'Hi,

Humphrey Dumpty,' he said.

He calls me Humphrey Dumpty
for fun.

I call him Lower-Your-Voice-A.J.
because of his loud voice.

'Hi, Og,' A.J. said.

Og answered with a friendly,
'BOING!'

'BOING-BOING!'
Andy said.

Then he hopped
across the room,
shouting, 'BOING-
BOING! I'M A FROG!'

'Quiet, Andy,' Garth told him.

A.J. leaned down close to Andy and said, 'Sssh!'

Andy said, 'Sssh!'

'Bedtime, Andy,' Garth's dad called from the hallway.

Andy said, 'Night-night, ham and frog.'

The boys played a game until Garth's dad called from the hallway again.

'Time to get washed and ready for bed, guys,' he said. 'You've got a big day tomorrow.'

Once Garth and A.J. had left, I told Og, 'We've got a big day tomorrow, too.'

This time, Og was silent.

Maybe he wished the treasure was in his tank instead of my cage.

I wanted to uncover the treasure to see what was inside, but I'd promised Garth I wouldn't peek.

It's always a good idea to keep a promise. I hopped on my wheel so I wouldn't think about the treasure.

I was spinning FAST-FAST-FAST when I saw the door to my cage open.

I wanted to see who was opening it, but my wheel was going so fast, I had to wait until it slowed down. While I waited, I saw the shadowy shape of a hand reach in and poke around the cage.

I had to see whose hand it was, so I hopped off the wheel and flipped head-over-paws across my bedding.

I must have been dizzy because everything was still spinning.

The hand picked up the small treasure chest. I tried to see whose hand it was, but now the chest blocked my view.

'Stop!' I squeaked as loudly as a small hamster can squeak. 'Stop right now!'

'Sssh!' was the only answer.

'Stop, thief!' I squeaked as my heart went THUMP-THUMP-THUMP.

No one answered. But I did smell something. Was it . . . chocolate?

'BOING-BOING!' Og called out as he splashed wildly in his tank.

Before I knew it, the hand had taken the treasure chest out of my cage and closed the door. I dashed forward to see who it was but it was too late. Garth's room was empty.

'Og, did you see the thief?' I asked.

Og didn't answer this time. I don't think he'd seen who it was. Neither had I.

I was unsqueakably upset.

The treasure chest was GONE-GONE-GONE!

★

'A thief was here!' I told Garth when he and A.J. came back, ready for bed. 'We have to find the thief!'

'Calm down, Humphrey Dumpty,' A.J. said. 'Sssh!'

'Goodnight, Humphrey,' Garth said.

He took off his glasses and got into his bed. A.J. got into the other bed in Garth's room.

'BOING-BOING!' Og said.

'Goodnight, Og,' Garth said.

I love humans but sometimes I wish they'd pay a little more attention.

The boys talked in the dark for a while. And soon I could tell by their breathing that they were asleep. But *I* didn't sleep the whole night.

Like most hamsters, I am usually wide awake at night. But I'm not usually so WORRIED-WORRIED-WORRIED.

It had been nice to have the treasure chest in my cage. But it was *not nice at all* to have it missing.

I imagined what would happen the next day. Everyone would try to find out where the treasure was by reading Garth's clues. One of my friends would be the first to get to my cage. But when that friend got there, the treasure would be missing.

I thought about how the winner would be disappointed.

I thought about how Garth would be disappointed.

Garth's parents would be disappointed, too.

But nobody would be more disappointed than me.

Early the next morning, Garth woke up A.J.

'Come on,' he said. 'We've got to get ready for the party. I've got a big surprise planned.'

'What is it?' A.J. asked.

'Wait and see,' Garth said.

Later, while A.J. was out of the room, I tried to tell Garth again that the treasure was missing.

'You sound excited, Humphrey,' he said. 'So am I! After all, you're the most important guest because you have the treasure!'

Except, of course, I hadn't.

The boys went downstairs to get ready for the party. 'I've got to do something, don't you think?' I asked Og.

'BOING-BOING-BOING!' he agreed.

Since the family was at home, I didn't dare go far from my cage. I decided to search for *new* treasure so the party wouldn't be ruined.

It's a secret, but I have a lock-that-doesn't-lock on my cage door. I can get in and out without any humans knowing it.

I jiggled the lock and the door opened. I was free!

It's a LONG-LONG-LONG way down to the floor for a small hamster and I didn't have much time. So I decided to stay close to my cage and explore the top of Garth's desk first.

There was a *lot* to see

on the top of Garth's desk.

The first thing I saw was a cup full
of pencils. But these weren't plain
pencils. They had amazing things on
top, like an orange pumpkin head,
a smiling monkey, a shiny star. One
pencil looked like a rocket ship!

Next to the pencil cup was a huge yellow smiling face. When I saw it, I smiled back.

'Hello,' I said, trying to be friendly.

Then I saw that the smiling face was really a clock.

'Never mind!' I said.

Behind the clock was a frame made of twigs with a picture of Garth and A.J. in it.

I wandered past a deck of cards and ran right into a tiny pink pig. The pig fell over and let out an 'Oink!'

'Sorry,' I said, and quickly moved on.

There were pads of paper, a large

blue feather and a pencil box with
the planets on it. I know about
planets from our lessons in Room 26.

I kept on walking and found
myself face to face with a row
of big dinosaurs with very large
teeth. They weren't real dinosaurs,
thank goodness. But they still were
unsqueakably scary to a small
hamster like me.

I scurried past a row of toy cars in bright colours. One was painted a shiny red and had no roof. It was just my size and I stopped to look at it.

I just touched the shiny red car with my paw when, suddenly, it lurched forward.

'VROOOM!' the car roared.

'Eeek!' I squeaked.

The car zipped across the desk, making wild turns. I ran for my life, zig-zagging ahead of it until I saw I was running straight towards the end of the desk! And it was a LONG-

LONG-LONG way
down to the floor.

To my left, was a
pencil case that was
taller than I am.

To my right, was the
front edge of the desk.
Eeek!

At the last second, I leaped up onto
the pencil case. The car zoomed past
me and flew off the end of the desk.
It sailed through the air and then
landed on Garth's soft bed.

'BOING-BOING!' Og said as I
caught my breath.

My heart was pounding, but I told him, 'Don't worry. I'm fine and so is the car!'

'BOING-BOING-BOING!' Og warned me.

He was right. I didn't have much time.

'I'll hurry,' I told him.

Then something caught my eye.
Something shiny and gold, like
treasure. It was a coin!

I hopped off the pencil case and
scampered towards it. When I sniffed
it, I realised that it wasn't a real coin,
but a chocolate wrapped in gold
paper.

Still, it was shiny and gold and my
friends all like chocolate.

I held it in my mouth, careful not
to bite down and make teeth marks,
and hurried back to my cage.

Og splashed loudly and called out,
'BOING-BOING!'

'I'll tell you all about it,' I said. But
I didn't have time because I heard
footsteps.

I dashed inside my cage and pulled
the door closed behind me.

I slipped the chocolate coin under

my bedding just as Garth came in.

'Time to go downstairs,' Garth said. 'The party's about to start.'

The Hunt Is On

Garth and his dad carried my cage and Og's tank outside to a table under a large umbrella.

'A.J., could you come and help me ice the cake?' Garth's mum asked. 'You can lick the spoon.'

'Yes, ma'am!' A.J. followed her in to the house.

Once he was gone, Garth said,

'We have to hide the clues before he comes back.'

Og and I watched as Garth and his dad put the little squares of paper all round the garden.

They put them in odd places, like a watering can and a little red wagon.

'Hurry, Dad,' Garth said.

Suddenly, I heard happy voices. My friends from Room 26 had arrived!

'Oh, Humphrey, I'm so glad you're here!' That was the voice of Miranda Golden.

I thought of her as Golden-Miranda because her hair was as golden as my fur.

'Hi, Humphrey! Hi, Og!' a giggly voice said. That had to be Stop-Giggling-Gail. It was hard for her to stop giggling once she got started.

'HI-HI-HI!' I answered.

Once the guests had arrived, Garth's mum called them into the garden for a funny race. First, each of my friends stood in a sack. Then they had to hold on to the sack while they hopped to the finish line.

I wish Og could have been in that race. He's GREAT-GREAT-GREAT at hopping.

But Gail and her friend Heidi
Hopper were good at hopping, too.
They won the race.

Next, my friends split up into pairs
and Garth's parents tied one kid's
right leg to the other kid's left leg.
Then they had to work together
to run to the finish line. It was

unsqueakably funny to see them try to run like that!

Seth and Tabitha won. They are good friends who are both good at sport.

There were other games, too, but it was hard for me to enjoy them. All I could think about was the treasure hunt.

Finally, Garth announced that the hunt would begin. 'There's *real treasure* for the first person who finds it,' he explained.

That was true. It just wasn't the treasure Garth had planned on.

Garth read out the first clue. 'Everyone knows you must water a flower. Tip me over, I'll give it a shower.'

My friends raced off in different directions.

'Og, I saw him put a clue in the watering can,' I squeaked. 'That must be it.'

I was right. Mandy, Richie and Seth all ran to the watering can at the same time.

Mandy reached in and pulled out the next clue.

'The sun is hot, as you will see. You'll be cooler under me.'

There were squeals of excitement as everyone raced to the umbrella over the table I was on.

A.J. had to stand on a chair to reach the next clue and read it.

'You'll find that you will never frown. If you let me go up and down.'

It took a little longer this time for my friends to solve that riddle, but I quickly got it.

'The swing!' I squeaked.

I don't think they understood me, but they all ran to the swing at the back of the garden.

Tabitha grabbed the clue first and read it.

'If going places is your goal, use me, for I am ready to roll!'

'It's the car,' Art shouted.

Art and some of my other friends headed for the driveway. But Heidi and Gail ran towards a little red wagon.

'That's it!' I shouted.

'BOING-BOING!' Og agreed.

Heidi reached into the wagon and pulled out the next clue.

'A-tisket, a-tasket. The last clue's in a basket.'

I must not have been paying attention when Garth and his dad hid that clue. I looked out at the garden.

I was confused. So were my friends.

A.J. and Richie ran towards a large plant in a basket. But when they reached in, there was no clue.

Miranda hurried to Garth's bicycle, which had a wire basket on the front. But when she reached in, there was no clue.

Seth and Tabitha ran to a basket of fruit on the food table. They searched and searched but there was no clue.

My friends all stopped and looked around the garden again.

Then Art spotted a tiny basket

hanging from a low tree branch. He reached inside and found the clue, which he read.

'You'll find the treasure – do not worry. Look for something cute and furry.'

My heart went THUMP-THUMP-THUMP. This time *I* was the clue.

At first, my friends just stood there.
I could tell they were thinking hard.

A.J. picked up Andy's teddy bear
from a chair. He looked and looked
but there was no treasure.

'Cute and furry,' I heard Miranda
whisper to Sayeh.

Suddenly, Sayeh's face lit up. I call
her Speak-Up-Sayeh because she's
so quiet in class. But this time her
voice was loud and clear as she said,
'Humphrey!'

Sayeh and Miranda raced to my
cage. While Miranda looked on the
outside of the cage, Sayeh opened
the door and reached inside.

'Humphrey, do you mind if I look

in your cage?' she asked.

'Help yourself,' I said.

She gently poked around in the bedding.

'I found the treasure!' she said as she held up the chocolate coin.

Garth rushed to her side. He was looking VERY-VERY-VERY confused.

'That's not the treasure!' he said.

Garth reached into my cage and poked around some more. Then he turned to face his friends.

'The real treasure is missing,' he said. 'This is fake treasure.'

Sayeh looked unsqueakably
confused.

Garth looked unsqueakably upset.

I was unsqueakably sorry that
everybody was so disappointed.

Mystery Solved

'What did you do with it, Humphrey?' Garth asked me. 'Where did you hide it?'

'I didn't!' I squeaked. 'The thief took it.'

'Humphrey's just a hamster,' Garth's dad said. 'What could he do?'

'You don't know Humphrey,' Garth said.

Some of my friends laughed.
They knew I'd had a lot of amazing
adventures.

'Humphrey wouldn't do anything
bad,' Miranda said.

'BOING!' Og added.

My other friends all agreed.

Garth shook his head. 'But how
could the real treasure disappear like

that? And how did the chocolate coin get into Humphrey's cage?'

'I'm happy with the treasure I found,' Sayeh said. 'Don't worry, Garth.'

But Garth was still upset. 'I don't know how that coin got in there. It was on my desk.'

'Do you think a thief came in and stole your treasure?' Garth's mum smiled. 'And then replaced it? That's silly.'

'No, it's not!' I squeaked.

'Somebody could have taken it while we were searching,' Garth said. 'We weren't looking at Humphrey's cage the whole time.'

'True,' Garth's dad said.

'False!' I said. 'You're WRONG-
WRONG-WRONG!'

Everybody laughed at my
squeaking. I wish they'd at least try
to understand me.

'Only Humphrey really knows
what happened,' Miranda said.

She was almost right. Og and I
were the only ones who knew that

the thief had stolen the treasure the night before.

She didn't know that we had no idea who the thief was.

I thought about who it could have been.

The only humans who were in the house were Garth, his mum, his dad, Andy and A.J.

Garth wouldn't have taken his own treasure. If he had, wouldn't he have told me?

Garth's mum and dad were too nice to steal anything.

A.J. wasn't a thief. But had he been playing a joke on Garth?

And Andy had been asleep in bed

when the treasure was stolen.

I looked at Garth's little brother.

He didn't look like a thief.

But he did look funny with
chocolate smeared all over his face.

'Andy! I told you, no chocolate
cake until later!' Garth's mum said
when she saw him. 'You sneaked
some chocolate last night, too.'

'Yum, chocolate,' Andy said.
'YUM!'

Garth said, 'Sssh!'

Andy said, 'Sssh!' right back.

The thief had smelled like chocolate. Andy loved chocolate. And he'd been eating it last night.

The thief had said 'Sssh!' Garth and A.J. said 'Sssh!' But Andy liked to say 'Sssh!' a *lot*.

Andy had been in the house last night. But now I knew he hadn't been in bed.

I raced to the front of my cage.

'You did it, Andy! You're the thief,' I squeaked. 'Turn yourself in!'

All my friends giggled at my

SQUEAK-SQUEAK-SQUEAKs.
But I didn't giggle.

'Andy is the thief!' I said. 'He did it!'

'Humphrey seems mad at Andy,' Garth said.

'Yes, he does,' Garth's mum said.

She turned to Andy. 'Did you take the treasure out of Humphrey's cage?'

Andy looked down at the ground.

'Yes,' he said softly.

'Why?' Garth asked.

'I like treasure,' Andy said.

Garth had another question. 'And did you put the chocolate coin in the cage?'

'I like chocolate,' Andy said.

It wasn't a real answer, but Garth didn't notice.

'Go get the treasure,' Garth's dad said. '*Now!*'

Andy went into the house and soon came back carrying the little treasure chest.

'Give it to Sayeh,' Garth's mum told him. 'And tell her you're sorry.'

Andy handed Sayeh the chest.

'Sorry,' he said.

He looked REALLY-REALLY-REALLY sorry, too.

Everyone gathered round while Sayeh opened the tiny chest.

'Oh!' she said as she reached inside. 'It's a gift card for Tilly's Toy Store!'

All my friends said, 'Oooh.'

Sayeh handed Andy the chocolate

coin. 'This is for you, Andy. Because you told the truth.'

Andy smiled happily, until his mum took the coin to save for later.

'Thanks for solving the mystery for us, Humphrey,' Garth's dad said. 'You're quite a treasure yourself.'

'BOING-BOING!' Og agreed.

'Og, you're a treasure, too,' Garth's dad laughed.

Garth's mum announced it was time for cake and ice cream so my friends ran off to the food table.

But Garth came straight back.

'Humphrey, I'm sorry I blamed you,' he said. 'I should have known that you'd never steal anything.'

He opened the door of my cage and put a small piece of carrot inside.

'Here's a treat for you,' he said.

Yum! That lovely orange carrot looked like sparkly golden treasure to me.

I hid it under the bedding in my cage for later on, when I'd have a treasure hunt all by myself.

'Thanks for making it a great party,' Garth said.

'You're welcome,' I replied. 'It was a GREAT-GREAT-GREAT party.'

And I REALLY-REALLY-REALLY meant it.

Have you read all my tiny tales?

See what unsqueakably exciting adventures I've had . .

Humphrey's Tiny Tales

My Pet Show PANIC!

BETTY G. BIRNEY

Humphrey's Tiny Tales

My Summer Fair SURPRISE!

BETTY G. BIRNEY

Humphrey's Tiny Tales

My Creepy-Crawly Camping
ADVENTURE!

BETTY G. BIRNEY

ff

Humphrey's Tiny Tales

My Great Big BIRTHDAY BASH!

BETTY G. BIRNEY

Dear friends,

Humans love their pets, and pets like me love their humans. I'm unsqueakably excited to share everything I've learned in Classroom 26 and beyond about the world of pets with you.

And hamsters aren't the only pets! Do you know how to look after a chinchilla? What is a puppy's favourite food? As well as learning top pet-care tips, you can tell me all about your pets in the special My Precious Pet section. I can't wait to meet them!

Your furry friend,

Humphrey

PET-tastic facts

WOOF!

LOTS
of fun
inside!

Humphrey's
World of Pets

Betty G. Birney

Look for my book of
unsqueakably funny jokes

With unsqueakably funny jokes from my readers – You!
Silly
Silly
Silly
HEE-HEE-HEE
Parp!!
Humphrey's
Ha-Ha-Ha
Joke Book
Betty G. Birney

Or why not try the
puzzles and games in my
fun-fun-fun activity
book!

Humphrey and his friends have been hard at work making a brand new FUN-FUN-FUN website just for you!

Play Humphrey's exciting new game, share your pet pictures, find fun crafts and activities, read Humphrey's very own diary and discover all the latest news from your favourite furry friend at:

www.funwithhumphrey.com